Disney
MICKEY
& FRIENDS

Fairy Tales
Storybook
Collection

This edition published by Parragon Books Ltd in 2014

Parragon Books Ltd
Chartist House
15–17 Trim Street
Bath BA1 1HA, UK
www.parragon.com

ISBN 978-1-4454-7899-9

Printed in China

Fairy Tales
Storybook
Collection

Bath · New York · Cologne · Melbourne · Delhi
Hong Kong · Shenzhen · Singapore · Amsterdam

Contents

Long, long ago, there was a place where the sun shone every day. It was called Happy Valley. Everything there was pretty and green and ... happy!

High on a hilltop overlooking the valley stood a castle. Inside were many beautiful things, but the most beautiful thing of all was a golden harp.

It was no ordinary harp, though. This harp sang sweetly and its magical music cast a spell of peace over Happy Valley.

One day, a mysterious shadow darkened the valley.

When it went away, the harp had disappeared.

Without the harp, the magic spell was broken.

Soon, the people grew sad and hungry.

Three farmers were sadder and hungrier than anyone

else – Farmer Mickey, Farmer Donald and Farmer Goofy.

They only had a slice of bread and a few beans between

them. They decided there was nothing left to do but trade

their cow for food.

So off Farmer Mickey went. But on his way to the market,

Mickey came upon an old man.

"Hello, Farmer Mickey," said the man. "Where are you off to?"

"I'm going to the market to sell my cow," Mickey explained.

The old man looked at the cow. "I'll give you these magical

beans for her. If you plant them under a full

moon, they will grow right up to the sky!"

Farmer Mickey was curious and

there was a full moon that night,

so he agreed to trade his cow

for the beans.

When Mickey returned home, he showed Donald and Goofy the beans.

"Three beans!" his friends cried angrily. "We can't live on three beans, Mickey!"

"They are magic beans," Mickey tried to explain. But his friends wouldn't listen.

Donald grabbed the beans and threw them on the ground. They bounced once, twice and then landed in a hole in the floor.

The three farmers crawled into bed hungrier than ever. They didn't know what they would do.

Then, under the bright moonlight, something strange happened. The beans began to grow. A stem formed and quickly turned into a huge stalk. The beanstalk climbed all the way into the sky, carrying the farmers' little house with it!

When the hungry farmers awoke, they looked out of the window. But they weren't in Happy Valley anymore! They were in a strange land on top of the clouds.

Mickey pointed to a giant castle in the distance. "Whoever lives there must have plenty of food. Maybe he'll share it with us."

The three friends ran to the castle. They helped one another climb the stairs and then slid under the door.

14

When they got inside, they spotted huge bowls and plates filled with food. They had never seen so much to eat in one place!

The farmers hurried to the table and started eating everything in sight.

Soon Mickey, Goofy and Donald were too full to eat another bite. Suddenly they heard a tiny voice call out to them from a box on the table.

"Who are you?" Mickey asked.

"It is I, the golden harp," said the voice. "A wicked giant stole me and brought me here to sing for him. The sound helps him sleep."

The farmers were frightened when they heard the word 'giant'. Just then, everything in the room started to shake. Heavy footsteps thundered towards them and a voice roared out, "Fee-fi-fo-fum!"

Mickey, Donald and Goofy hid behind a sugar bowl. The giant entered the room. He was taller than ten men and looked stronger than forty!

The giant started to make himself a big meal. As he reached for the sugar, the three friends scurried to find new hiding places. Mickey hid in the bread. But the giant used the bread to make a sandwich and Mickey got stuck inside! The giant was about to take a bite when he noticed the farmer wriggling around.

"Gotcha!" the giant cried, grabbing Mickey.

Then he scooped up Donald and Goofy and dropped all three into the box where the golden harp was being kept.

The giant grabbed the harp, locked the box and slipped the key into his pocket. He didn't notice that Mickey had managed to escape.

The giant sat down on a nearby chair and placed the harp on the table in front of him. The harp sang sweetly and soon lulled him to sleep.

When Mickey heard the giant snoring, he climbed down a piece of thread. Then, ever so carefully, he reached into the giant's pocket and took the key. The giant mumbled something, but he did not wake up.

As quickly as he could, Mickey let his friends out of the box and grabbed the harp. But as they made their way to the front door, the giant opened one eye.

"Come back here!" he roared.

Goofy and Donald ran away with the harp.

Mickey knew he had to distract the giant.

"You can't catch me!" he yelled. The angry

giant ran towards Mickey, who dived under a rug.

"Over here!" Mickey said, but the

giant was not fast enough to catch him.

Mickey ran towards an open window.

"So long!" he cried as he jumped outside

and chased after his friends. The giant

thundered after him, shouting for the

farmers to bring back his harp.

The ground shook with every step the giant took but the farmers kept going. They climbed down the beanstalk as fast as they could. Donald and Goofy reached the ground first.

While Mickey hurried the rest of the way, his friends grabbed a saw and began to cut down the stem.

But the giant had followed them and was climbing down, down, down. Donald and Goofy kept sawing.

At last the beanstalk began to wobble. Finally it toppled over.

The giant crashed to the ground and lay still.

With the giant gone, the farmers took the golden harp back to the castle on the hilltop. Happy Valley was a very cheerful place once more. And no one was more pleased than the three brave friends – Mickey, Donald and Goofy. They had saved the harp and Happy Valley!

Daisylocks

In a pretty little cottage deep in the woods lived the Three Bears – Papa Bear, Mama Bear and Baby Bear.

"I wish someone would come and visit us," Papa Bear said in his great big voice.

"I think the other animals are scared of us," Mama Bear said in her medium-sized voice.

"I'm too small to scare anybody," Baby Bear said in his wee little voice.

One morning, right before breakfast, the Three Bears decided to go for a walk.

On the other side of the woods there lived a girl named Daisylocks. Just before eating her breakfast, she decided to go for a walk, too.

Out in the woods, the Three Bears and Daisylocks passed right by each other. The only one who noticed was Baby Bear. Everyone else was too busy enjoying the fresh air.

After walking for a while, Daisylocks came upon the Three Bears' home. "Oh, look! A pretty little cottage!" she cried.

Daisylocks knew she shouldn't go in without being invited. But she tried the front door anyway.

"It's unlocked!" she exclaimed. "I'll be a good neighbour and make sure nothing is wrong."

Daisylocks opened the door and walked into a cosy kitchen, leaving a trail of muddy footprints behind her. Something smelled delicious. There, sitting on the table, were three bowls of porridge – a great big bowl, a medium-sized bowl and a wee little bowl.

Daisylocks hadn't eaten breakfast yet and she was hungry! So she helped herself to the porridge in the great big bowl. "Wow!" she gasped. "That porridge is too hot!"

Daisylocks' mouth stung from the hot porridge but she was still hungry. So she decided to try the porridge in the medium-sized bowl.

"Ick," Daisylocks cried. "That's too cold."

Finally Daisylocks tasted the porridge in the wee little bowl.
It was just right and she ate it all!

Daisylocks finished eating and left the table so quickly she
didn't even notice that she'd spilled some porridge on the floor.

Next, she went into the living room. There she found three chairs – a great big chair, a medium-sized chair and a wee little chair.

Poor Daisylocks' feet were tired from all that walking in the woods. The chairs looked very comfortable so she decided to make herself at home. She climbed into the great big chair, slid her feet into the great big slippers next to it and frowned. The chair was hard as a rock. It made her tail feathers hurt!

Daisylocks climbed into the medium-sized chair next.

But it was too soft. She couldn't see over all the cushions!

Daisylocks sank into them and almost got stuck.

Finally Daisylocks tried the wee little chair. It was just right! She leaned back, but ... CRASH! The chair tipped over and broke.

"Oh, well," Daisylocks said as she dusted herself off. "I guess it wasn't just right after all."

Daisylocks decided to see what was in the next room. There she found three beds – a great big bed, a medium-sized bed and a wee little bed.

Daisylocks yawned. She was feeling rather sleepy, so she climbed up into the great big bed. It was too hard.

"The mattress must be extra firm," she said.

Next Daisylocks tried the medium-sized bed. But when she lay down, she sank into the mattress.

"Too squishy," she said, getting up again.

Finally she went over to the wee little bed and got in.

"Not too hard. Not too soft," she said. "Yes, this is just right."

And wrapping her arm round the teddy bear on the bed, she pulled up the covers and fell into a deep, deep sleep.

Daisylocks had only been asleep for a few minutes when the Three Bears came home. They noticed Daisylocks's muddy footprints right away.

"I wonder who is in our house!" cried Papa Bear.
The Three Bears decided to investigate.

First, they went into the kitchen.

"Someone has been eating my porridge!"

Papa Bear bellowed in his great big voice.

"Someone has been eating my porridge!"

Mama Bear cried in her medium-sized voice.

Baby Bear looked into his empty bowl.

"Someone has been eating my porridge, too,"

he said in his wee little voice. "Every last bit is gone!"

The Three Bears went into the living room.

"Someone has been sitting in my chair," Papa Bear roared in his great big voice. "My slippers have been moved!"

"Someone has been sitting in my chair, too!" Mama Bear wailed in her medium-sized voice. "There are cushions everywhere!"

Baby Bear looked at the pieces of his chair.

"Someone has been sitting in my chair," he said in his wee little voice. "And now it's broken!"

The Three Bears followed the muddy footprints into the bedroom.

Papa Bear looked at the rumpled blankets on his bed. "Someone has been sleeping in my bed!" he growled in his great big voice.

Mama Bear looked at the pillows on the floor. "Someone has been sleeping in my bed, too!" she groaned in her medium-sized voice.

"Someone has been sleeping in my bed!" Baby Bear said in his wee little voice. "And there she is!"

Mama Bear and Papa Bear hurried over.

All the noise had woken Daisylocks. She opened her eyes and saw the Three Bears staring at her.

"Eek!" she shrieked.

Daisylocks leaped out of the wee little bed. She raced down the stairs, past the broken chair and empty porridge bowl. Then she threw open the door and ran away from the cottage as fast as her feet could carry her.

The Three Bears watched Daisylocks run away and then cleaned everything up. Some new friends they had made on their walk were coming for a visit!

And Daisylocks? Well, she decided she'd never go into anyone's house without being invited again!

The Prince
and the
Pauper

48

Once upon a time, there was a kindly king who ruled with fairness and generosity. His son, the prince, was busy with his studies but he loved the kingdom, too. It was a time of great peace and the people of the land were very happy.

But then the king grew sick and could no longer watch over his people.

49

The greedy leader of the king's guards, Captain Pete, saw the king's illness as his chance to get rich. Day after day, the captain and his soldiers took food and money from the people of the kingdom.

One very cold morning, a peasant named Mickey watched as the royal coach drove past him. Mickey's dog, Pluto, spotted some sausages hanging from the back and ran after them. The coach disappeared through the palace gates with Pluto following it.

"Stop!" Mickey shouted as he ran after his dog. "Come back!" But it was too late. The gates had shut behind Pluto.

When Mickey got to the gate, he asked if he could go inside to get his dog. The guard was about to say no when he looked at the peasant's face. "Your Majesty," the guard said, gasping. He quickly waved Mickey inside.

Mickey didn't notice what the guard had called him. He just wanted his dog back.

Meanwhile, inside the palace, the prince was sitting through a boring history lesson with Professor Horace. To amuse himself, he took out a peashooter and aimed it at his valet, Donald.

WHACK! The prince landed a shot right on Donald's head. WHACK! Another one hit the valet's bottom.

It wasn't until the third pea struck him that Donald finally fired back. Unfortunately, his aim was a bit off. Instead of hitting the young prince, he hit the professor!

Professor Horace was about to scold Donald and the prince
when there was a noise outside. The prince ran to the window
and looked down. Captain Pete was holding a bag with
someone trapped inside. It was Mickey! The captain had found
him wandering around and captured him. The prince ordered
Pete to let the captive out of the bag and send him inside.

Pete did as he was told, but the young pauper was so busy looking at everything around him that he soon got lost. Shiny suits of armour lined the walls. Crystal chandeliers hung from the ceiling. The whole palace gleamed. Mickey grinned with delight at the sight of his own reflection on the polished floor.

He took a quick look around to make sure no one was watching, then kicked up his heels and danced a little jig.

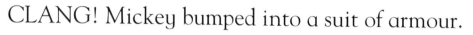

CLANG! Mickey bumped into a suit of armour.
The helmet fell off and landed on his head. As he
staggered around in the sudden darkness,
Mickey bumped into another suit of
armour, which toppled over on to
another one, which toppled
over on to another....

Just then the prince entered the hall and another helmet
fell down – on to his head! Neither the prince nor the pauper
could see where they were going. They walked blindly until
– BANG! – they crashed into each other.
Slowly, they lifted up the fronts
of their helmets.

"You look just like
me!" they shouted
in unison.

The prince couldn't believe his luck. This was just the chance he had been waiting for! Now he could leave the boring palace and no one would know. He quickly convinced Mickey to trade places with him. To Mickey, the idea of living in a luxurious palace as a prince sounded amazing. What harm could it do? They swapped clothes and the prince headed for the door. "I'll be back in the blink of an eye," he promised.

The prince made it outside and hurried away to enjoy his day as a pauper. He tried playing fetch with some dogs but they chased him over a fence.

He tried to join a snowball fight but it was three against one. Finally, he went to the market. There he saw one of the captain's guards stealing food from poor people.

"Halt! I am the prince," he cried and held up his royal ring to prove it. Then he climbed on top of the cart and gave the food to the hungry peasants.

The guard took one look at the prince's ring and rushed back to tell Pete what had happened. When Captain Pete heard the news, he came up with a plan. He would get rid of the real prince and make the fake one do whatever he demanded.

Meanwhile, Mickey's friend Goofy had found the prince walking about town and taken him to his house. A while later, the church bells tolled throughout the land. The king had died.

The prince told Goofy that he was not Mickey, but the new ruler. He showed Goofy his ring. "I must go to the palace right away," he said. "It is my duty to take over as king." Then he leaped out of his chair and headed for the door.

But Captain Pete was waiting for him.

Pete's guards quickly captured the prince. They took him to the palace and threw him into the dungeon with Donald.

"I see your royal ring," Pete said from outside the prince's cell, "but it won't do you any good. As soon as the pauper is crowned king, I shall unmask him as an imposter and rule the kingdom myself!" And with an evil laugh, he left.

The situation looked hopeless for the prince – and for the entire kingdom.

Just then, a strange-looking guard came to the dungeon door. It was Goofy! He knocked out the guard and handed Donald the keys to the cell. "Sit tight, little buddy," Goofy told the prince.

While Donald struggled with the lock, Goofy kept an eye out for more guards. Finally, the cell door swung open. Goofy, Donald and the prince took off, with Pete's guards close behind.

Meanwhile, Mickey was trying to avoid being crowned king. He knew that Captain Pete would keep stealing from the people of the kingdom, so he stopped the ceremony. "I'm the prince. So whatever I order must be done, right?" Mickey asked the man who was about to crown him. The man nodded and Mickey ordered the guards to seize Pete.

But Pete was ready for this. "He is not the prince!" yelled the wicked captain. "He's an imposter. Seize him!"

"*I'm* not an imposter, though," came a voice from a high balcony. It was the real prince!

Everyone gasped and looked up as the prince swung to the ground on a chandelier. Swords slashed and fists flew as Mickey and his friends struggled against Pete's guards. Pluto even took a bite out of Pete's trousers!

Soon the fight was over. The evil captain was arrested and the prince was crowned king.

The kingdom was once again in kind, caring hands. With Mickey and Goofy by his side, the new king ruled happily ever after.

Little Red Riding Minnie

Once upon a time, there was a kindhearted girl who was loved by all who knew her. Her grandmother had made her a cape of red wool as a gift. The girl wore it so often that her family and friends began to call her Little Red Riding Minnie.

One day, Little Red Riding Minnie learned that her grandmother was sick with a bad cold. She decided to bake a batch of her famous oat-chocolate-chip cookies. Those were sure to make her grandmother feel better!

After the cookies had cooled, Little Red Riding Minnie put them in a tin. Then she packed some super-strong menthol cough drops in another tin. She thought her grandmother could probably use some of those, too.

Little Red Riding Minnie put both tins into her basket and set out for her grandmother's house.

The route took Little Red Riding Minnie through the centre of town – right down Main Street, which was a very busy shopping area.

Little Red Riding Minnie loved saying hello to the shopkeepers as she passed. She was enjoying her walk very much.

Then, just as she passed the post office, who should jump out of an alley and block her path but Big Bad Pete!

"Hello, Red,"
he said with a smirk.
"And where might
you be headed with
that basket?"

Now Big Bad Pete
was known to everyone
around town as a scoundrel.
He was certainly the last person
Little Red Riding Minnie would have wanted to meet on
her way to her grandmother's house. But Little Red Riding
Minnie tried to be polite to everyone and that included
Big Bad Pete!

"Well, if you must know," Little Red Riding Minnie replied, hugging her basket tightly, "I'm bringing some of my famous oatmeal-chocolate-chip cookies to my grandmother. She has a terrible cold. Now, if you'll excuse me...."

And with that, Little Red Riding Minnie hurried away.

As Big Bad Pete watched her go, his mouth began to water. Little Red Riding Minnie's oatmeal-chocolate-chip cookies *were* famous – famously delicious!

Big Bad Pete had to get his hands on those cookies, even if it meant tricking Little Red Riding Minnie.

So, while Little Red Riding Minnie continued along Main Street, stopping to window-shop here and talk to shopkeepers there, Big Bad Pete ducked down an alley, raced along the side streets and zipped through some back gardens.

Big Bad Pete arrived at Little Red Riding Minnie's grandmother's house ahead of Little Red Riding Minnie. He knew he had to come up with a plan.

As he hurried up the front path, Big Bad Pete spotted the grandmother's washing hanging out to dry in the garden. "Hmmm ... " he said.

Big Bad Pete grabbed the clean clothes and hid behind the house. He would be ready for Little Red Riding Minnie when she arrived!

Minutes later, Little Red Riding Minnie skipped up the front path towards her grandmother's front door. She was singing to herself and didn't notice anything unusual.

Before she could knock, Big Bad Pete jumped out from behind a bush. He was disguised in her grandmother's clothes!

"Oh, hello, Little Red Riding Minnie," Big Bad Pete squeaked, trying to sound like her grandmother. "Have you come to pay your grandmother a visit?"

"Why … uh … yes," Little Red Riding Minnie stammered. Grandmother's cold must be very bad indeed, she thought. She looks awful and I have never heard her sound so squeaky!

Little Red Riding Minnie looked more closely at her grandmother and started to notice some peculiar things. Something was definitely not right!

"Grandmother," Little Red Riding Minnie said, "what big ears you have!"

"All the better to hear you with, my dear," Big Bad Pete replied in his best grandmother voice.

"And what big eyes you have!" Little Red Riding Minnie exclaimed.

Big Bad Pete crept closer to her. "All the better to see you with, my dear," he squeaked.

"And what big
teeth you have!"
Little Red Riding
Minnie continued.

Big Bad Pete moved
even closer. Now he was
right over her. "All the
better to eat your famous
oat-chocolate-chip
cookies with, my dear!" he shouted.

And with that, Big Bad Pete snatched a tin out of
Little Red Riding Minnie's basket, threw off his disguise
and began to laugh wickedly.

"Ah-ha-ha-ha! I tricked you! Now your cookies are all mine!"

As Little Red Riding Minnie looked on, Big Bad Pete pulled off the lid of the tin, threw his head back and emptied the entire contents into his mouth.

Too bad for Big Bad Pete … it was the wrong tin.

It took only a few seconds before the super-strong menthol cough drops began to work their magic. Big Bad Pete's face turned bright pink and his eyes got large. He ran down the front path and away from Little Red Riding Minnie.

He needed to find a drink of water!

Just then, Little Red Riding Minnie's real grandmother opened the door.

"Oh, hello, dear," she said as she dabbed at her nose with a handkerchief. "Is everything all right?"

"Oh, yes, Grandmother," Little Red Riding Minnie replied. "Everything is just fine."

So Little Red Riding Minnie had a pleasant visit with her grandmother, who greatly enjoyed the oat-chocolate-chip cookies.

Little Red Riding Minnie left the recipe with her grandmother and walked home, stopping to say hello to some friends along the way.

Meanwhile, Big Bad Pete decided that Little Red Riding Minnie's cookies were not all they were cracked up to be. As he drank bucket after bucket of water, he vowed never to scare anyone for their famously-delicious cookies ever again.

Pied Piper
Mickey

TAILOR

Long ago, there was a small town called Hamelin. It was filled with cosy wooden houses and hardworking townspeople. But there was one problem: bugs. Thousands and thousands of bugs!

There were bugs in the bedrooms and bugs in the barns. They climbed up the walls of the houses and down into the wells. They even took over the inn and had all-night bug parties.

"There are beetles in my pies," the baker complained.

"I have ants in my pants," cried the tailor.

The people of Hamelin tried everything. They tried bug swatters. They tried fancy traps. They even tried leading the bugs out of town with trails of crumbs. But nothing made the bugs go away.

One day, a stranger appeared in town. He wore colourful clothes and a pointy red hat. Under his arm was a long silver pipe.

"Good morning!" he called merrily. "I'm Pied Piper Mickey. I can charm any creature with my magical music. I heard all about your problem and I can help. I'll rid your town of bugs for good."

A cheer went up from the townspeople.

"And I will do it for only a thousand coins," Pied Piper Mickey said to the mayor.

"Oh, very well," grumbled the mayor. He was not very generous and hated to part with money, but he was out of ideas.

It was a deal.

Pied Piper Mickey went straight to the town square. He put his pipe to his mouth, closed his eyes and began to play a song.

The music was loud and screechy. Everyone covered their ears and ran away. But the bugs loved it!

As Pied Piper Mickey played, bugs came from every corner of the town. Green bugs, red bugs, speedy bugs and slow bugs all gathered around.

Pied Piper Mickey led a parade of bugs down the cobblestoned street and over the bridge. Every single bug in town danced along behind him, enjoying the music. They had never heard anything like it before.

Pied Piper Mickey led the bugs to the water. Then, as he continued to play, Pied Piper Mickey jumped in. The bugs happily followed, splashing and singing as they floated away, down the river and right out of town.

"Hooray for Pied Piper Mickey!" the people of Hamelin cheered.

They picked him up and carried him on their shoulders.

"Can I have my thousand coins now?" Pied Piper Mickey asked.

The mayor frowned. It had only taken Pied Piper Mickey

a few minutes to get rid of the bugs. That hardly seemed worth

a thousand coins.

"Here's fifty," the mayor offered.

"But our deal was for a thousand coins!" Pied Piper Mickey cried.

"And now it is fifty," replied the mayor.

"Oh, is that so?" Pied Piper Mickey said. He winked at the townspeople and put his pipe to his mouth again.

Pied Piper Mickey began playing the strange, screechy music again. The townspeople looked around nervously. What if the piper brought back all the bugs?

But only one bug appeared. A single gnat flew into the town square and landed on the mayor.

The townspeople laughed.

But Pied Piper Mickey just shrugged and kept playing. Soon, a few more bugs arrived. Some of them buzzed around the heads of the townspeople. Others went into the sweet shop and started taking lollipops and other sweet treats.

"Fine, I'll give you a hundred coins," the mayor said.

"Nope," said Pied Piper Mickey.

Beetles and caterpillars joined hands and danced. An orchestra of crickets took a break from practising to come to Hamelin to hear the music. It was a party!

In no time at all, bugs were flying, crawling and hopping all over town. Even the luna moths woke up from their daytime naps to listen to Pied Piper Mickey play.

"I'll give you six hundred," the mayor offered as he dodged a bumblebee.

"You know," Pied Piper Mickey said, "these bugs have a lot of friends who I'm sure would love to visit Hamelin."

"That's as high as I'm going to go," the mayor said.

Pied Piper Mickey just kept playing.

At last the mayor gave in. He shoved handfuls of gold coins at Pied Piper Mickey.

"Here! Take your thousand coins! Please, no more bugs!"

"Sure," Pied Piper Mickey replied. He stopped playing.

"For another thousand coins, I'll even take the bugs away again."

The mayor knew he had no choice. He paid Pied Piper Mickey.

"Whew," the mayor said. "You drive a hard bargain."

"It's only fair," Pied Piper Mickey said. "Maybe next time you'll stick to your end of the deal."

Pied Piper Mickey put the gold coins in his pocket. "Goodbye, everyone," he called. Then he tipped his hat and began to play another screechy tune.

Once again, he made his way across the bridge and towards the river. As he left town, every last bug followed him.

Well, almost every bug.

Pied Piper Mickey left one behind, just for the mayor.

And that was the last time the people of Hamelin ever saw Pied Piper Mickey – or any other bugs.

The Three Musketeers

Once upon a time, there lived three young friends named Mickey, Donald and Goofy. The friends dreamed of being like their greatest heroes – the Musketeers. The Musketeers were the strongest, bravest and cleverest soldiers in France. And they lived by the words: All for one and one for all!

Mickey and his friends were willing to do anything to become Musketeers. They even worked at the Musketeers' headquarters. They hoped that Captain Pete, head of the Musketeers, would notice them.

But Captain Pete had plans of his own – evil plans. Pete wanted to become king of France.

Captain Pete had hired the Beagle Boys to kidnap

Princess Minnie. With the princess out of the way, Pete could

claim the throne.

One day Princess Minnie was having tea with Lady Daisy.

As she went out to the garden, the Beagle Boys pushed a safe

off the balcony. They just missed the princess!

When Captain Pete found out what had happened, he was furious!

"I didn't say 'drop a safe', I said, 'keep her safe!'"

Pete turned to his lieutenant, Clarabelle. "Throw these clowns into the pit!"

Just then a messenger delivered an angry letter from Princess Minnie. It seemed Pete wasn't the only one who was upset.

"I want bodyguards," Princess Minnie told Pete. "Musketeer bodyguards!"

Pete knew that real Musketeers would interfere with his plan. Luckily, he had an idea.

"I've got the very men for you, Princess," Captain Pete promised.

Pete marched out to the courtyard. "You three are going to be Musketeers!" he told Mickey, Goofy and Donald.

Later that day, Mickey and his friends were escorting Princess Minnie and Lady Daisy on a royal trip. But the Beagle Boys were waiting for them.

As the royal coach passed by their hiding place, the Beagle Boys leaped on it.

Mickey was ready to fight, but Donald was scared and jumped into the coach.

"Get back out there, you coward," Minnie scolded.

Minnie pushed Donald out and he landed in the mud. He watched helplessly as Mickey and Goofy tried to fight off the Beagle Boys. The kidnappers quickly outwitted Goofy. And Mickey was no match for the big bullies.

Soon the Beagle Boys made their escape with Princess Minnie and Lady Daisy still in the royal coach.

But Mickey wasn't ready to give up. "Pete made us Musketeers, remember? That means it's our job to save the princess!"

The Musketeers found the coach near a deserted tower.
But when Mickey tried to open the tower door, it was stuck.

"Let me give it a go," Goofy said. Goofy ran at it as hard
as he could. The door swung open and he raced inside.

As he ran up the stairs, Goofy accidentally knocked things
out of the window. That gave him an idea. With his friends close
behind, Goofy knocked the kidnappers out of the window too.

The Musketeers escorted Princess Minnie and Lady Daisy back to the castle. As Goofy stood guard outside Princess Minnie's room, he saw a familiar shadow.

"Help me, Musketeer Goofy," a voice said. Goofy followed the shadow out of the palace. But it wasn't Mickey at all. Clarabelle had tricked Goofy! She quickly tied him up and dragged him away.

Meanwhile, Donald was also patrolling the palace. But when he spotted the Beagle Boys, he dived into a suit of armour and hid.

The Beagle Boys walked past Donald without even seeing him!

Mickey couldn't believe it when he found Donald in the suit of armour.

Donald told Mickey that he had heard the Beagle Boys talking about their plan to kidnap Princess Minnie again.

Mickey was shocked. His friends weren't really Musketeers.

It had all been a lie! "Well, lie or no lie, Musketeers don't run from danger," Mickey said to himself. Then he took off to find Captain Pete.

But Captain Pete found him first. With one blow, he knocked Mickey out. Then he locked him in a cage and carried him to a remote island prison.

Pete chained Mickey to a wall deep in the dungeon.

"Looks like this is the end of the line," Pete said.

"My friends will come for me," Mickey shot back.

"Oh, sure," Pete replied. "Face it! You're on your own!"

Suddenly, water began to pour into the dungeon.
Soon it would be flooded.

"See you later, Mickey," Captain Pete said as he
swept out of the room.

Mickey wasn't the only Musketeer in danger. Clarabelle was about to throw Goofy off a bridge! But as she bragged about Pete's plans for Mickey, the bridge gave way.

Clarabelle and Goofy plunged over the side, right into a boat that was being rowed by Donald!

Goofy knew they had to save Mickey. "It's all for one and one for all," he reminded Donald. Donald was still scared, but he agreed to go along.

Meanwhile, the water in Mickey's cell was rising. Mickey hadn't been able to break free from his chains. Then, just when it looked as if all hope was lost, Goofy and Donald arrived. They quickly freed Mickey and got him to safety.

The Three Musketeers raced off to save the princess.

At the opera, Pete told Minnie, "I'll be your bodyguard tonight." But then he bundled Daisy and Minnie into a large sack and gave it to two of the Beagle Boys.

Then the smallest Beagle Boy, dressed as Princess Minnie, stepped onstage. "My loyal subjects," the fake princess said. "Due to the stress of being a princess, I now present your new ruler – King Pete!"

Suddenly, Mickey
appeared. The audience sat
in shock as the opera began
– and a sword fight broke
out onstage!

Mickey had just freed
Minnie and Daisy when
Captain Pete joined the fight.

"It's over," Pete said.
"And you're alone."

"Wanna bet?" Mickey said, looking up. Goofy and Donald were
on their way! They had just defeated the Beagle Boys backstage.
Together, they knocked Captain Pete out and put an end to
his evil plan.

And that is how Princess Minnie came to make all three friends her Royal Musketeers!

Mickey, Donald and Goofy could hardly believe it. They might not be the biggest, bravest or smartest of all, but by working together they had made their dreams come true.

As the crowd cheered, Mickey couldn't help shouting, "All for one … "

And everyone – even Princess Minnie – called, " … and one for all!"

Little Red Hen

One day, the Little Red Hen was walking in the garden when she found a grain of wheat. "Oh, my," she said. "This is very exciting. I will plant it and reap it and grind it and bake it. Then I'll have some bread to eat with my tea."

On her way to the field, the Little Red Hen walked past Donald Duck. He was resting in a hammock.

"Look what I found!" she said to him. The Little Red Hen held up the grain. "I am going to plant it and grow wheat for bread. Will you help me?"

"Not I," Donald Duck said and waved her away. "I've come to the farm for a holiday, not to work. I would like to just lie here and sleep. Perhaps someone else will help you turn your grain into bread."

So the Little Red Hen wished Donald well and went on her way.

Next, the Little Red Hen ran into Pluto.

"Will you help me plant this grain of wheat?" she asked.

But Pluto didn't even look up.

He was too busy digging a hole to bury his bone.

So the Little Red Hen went on her way again.

Then the Little Red Hen saw Donald Duck's nephews –
Huey, Dewey and Louie.

"Will you help me plant this grain of wheat?" she asked.

"We can't," they said. "We're playing."

"Well then, I will plant it myself," she said.

And she did.

The grain of wheat grew and soon it was ready to reap.

"Will you help me reap the wheat?" the Little Red Hen asked Donald Duck.

"Not I," he said. "I am sunbathing. I would like to just lie here and sleep."

The Little Red Hen turned to Huey, Dewey and Louie.

"Will you help me reap the wheat?" she asked the three boys.

"We can't. We are playing a game of leap-duck," Huey explained.

The Little Red Hen called to Pluto, but he was still busy digging his hole and she could not get his attention.

"Well then, I will reap the wheat myself," said the Little Red Hen.

And she did.

While Donald Duck slept, Huey, Dewey and Louie played their game and Pluto dug a hole, the Little Red Hen walked out to the field.

The Little Red Hen looked around. Vegetables grew everywhere. Cabbage was waiting to be picked. Carrots were starting to poke through the soil. In a row of its own, a single stalk of wheat was waiting to be reaped.

With a flick of her wrist, the Little Red Hen cut the wheat. Then she gathered it up and headed to the mill, where the wheat would be ground into flour she could use to make her bread.

On her way to the mill, the Little Red Hen passed Donald Duck.

"Will you help me take this wheat to the mill?" she asked.

Donald Duck yawned. "Not I," he said. "I am swimming, as you can see."

The Little Red Hen went to find Donald Duck's nephews.

"Will you help me take this wheat to the mill?" she asked them.

"We can't," Dewey told her. "We are helping Pluto find his bone."

"Well then, I will do it myself," she said.

And she did.

The Little Red Hen went up the hill to Mickey Mouse's mill. Within the hour she had some flour.

"Now, who will help me make the flour into dough?" the Little Red Hen asked when she returned.

"Sorry," said Louie. "We are chasing butterflies."

Next, the Little Red Hen went looking for Pluto. But he was still looking for his bone! He had hidden it so well that he couldn't find it.

"Perhaps Donald Duck will help," the Little Red Hen said.

The Little Red Hen found Donald Duck leaning against a tree.

"Will you help me make this flour into dough?" she asked.

"Not I," mumbled Donald Duck, whose eyes were closed.

"I am reading a book."

"Well then, I will make the dough myself," said the Little Red Hen.

And she did.

The Little Red Hen made the dough, shaped it into a neat loaf and put it in the oven. Soon the whole cottage smelled of freshly baked bread.

When the loaf was golden brown, she took it out of the oven and set it on the windowsill.

While the bread cooled, the Little Red Hen got out a checked tablecloth, some butter, a jar of strawberry jam and a jug of creamy milk. Finally, everything was ready.

"And now," she called, "who will help me eat the bread?"

Donald Duck dropped his book and raced towards the cottage.

"I will!" he exclaimed, licking his lips.

Pluto left his hole and barked happily. He ran towards the cottage, too.

"We will!" shouted Huey, Dewey and Louie, leaving their balls, bats and butterfly nets all in a heap.

"No," said the Little Red Hen. "When I asked you to help me make the bread, you were too busy. I planted the grain, reaped the wheat, brought the wheat to the mill and turned the flour into dough all by myself. And now I will eat the bread by myself, too."

And she did.

Nursery Rhymes

Hey, diddle, diddle

Hey, diddle, diddle,

The cat and the fiddle,

The cow jumped over the moon;

The little dog laughed to see such sport,

And the dish ran away with the spoon.

Mary had a little lamb

Mary had a little lamb,

Its fleece was white as snow,

And everywhere that Mary went,

The lamb was sure to go.

It followed her to school one day,

Which was against the rules;

It made the children laugh and play

To see a lamb at school.

Little Jack Horner

Little Jack Horner sat in a corner,

Eating a Christmas pie.

He put in his thumb, pulled out a plum,

And said, "What a good boy am I!"

Humpty Dumpty

Humpty Dumpty sat on a wall,

Humpty Dumpty had a great fall.

All the king's horses and all the king's men

Couldn't put Humpty together again.

Hickory, dickory, dock

Hickory, dickory, dock,

The mouse ran up the clock.

The clock struck one;

The mouse ran down.

Hickory, dickory, dock.

Jack and Jill

Jack and Jill went up the hill

To fetch a pail of water.

Jack fell down and broke his crown,

And Jill came tumbling after.

Up Jack got, and home did trot,

As fast as he could caper.

He went to bed to mend his head

With vinegar and brown paper.

Little Miss Muffet

Little Miss Muffet

Sat on a tuffet,

Eating her curds and whey.

Along came a spider,

Who sat down beside her,

And frightened Miss Muffet away!

Georgie Porgie

Georgie Porgie, pudding and pie,

Kissed the girls and made them cry.

When the boys came out to play,

Georgie Porgie ran away.

Little Boy Blue

Little Boy Blue,

Come blow your horn,

The sheep's in the meadow,

The cow's in the corn.

Where is the boy

Who looks after the sheep?

He's under a haystack,

Fast asleep.

Will you wake him?

No, not I.

For if I do,

He's sure to cry.

Diddle diddle dumpling

Diddle diddle dumpling, my son John

Went to bed with his stockings on.

One shoe off and one shoe on,

Diddle diddle dumpling, my son John.